A Bloody Nuisance

Will Burke was the type who tends to wear on people's nerves. He wants to be friendly, but ends up being irritating.

He tries too hard.

Sandy Frenton is a female version of Will. As was often heard in the places they frequented, "They're a couple of bloody nuisances!"

That must have given somebody an idea. It wasn't meant to be taken literally.

Sgt. Andy Betts is assigned the case. It's his first homicide. His ability with this one could make or break his being on the next promotions list. His experience is with the academy and a lot of reading.

A bit of investigation told Andy there was something more behind the murders. Something sinister.

Contents

About the Author

CD Moulton has traveled extensively over much of the world both in the music business, where he was a rock guitarist, songwriter and arranger and in an import/export business. He has been everything from a bar owner to auto salvage (junkyard) manager, longshoreman to high steel worker, orchid grower to landscaper, tropical fish farmer to commercial fisherman. He started writing books in 1983 and has published more than 200 books as of January 1, 2014. His most popular books to date are about research with orchids, though much of his science fiction and fantasy work has proven popular. He wrote the CD Grimes, PI series and the Det. Nick Storie series, Clint Faraday series and many other works.

He now resides in Puerto Armuelles, Panamá, where he writes books, plays music with friends, does research with orchids and medicinal plants – and pursues his favorite ways to spend his time: beach bum and roaming the mountain jungles doing his botanical research.

He offers the free e-book, *Fading Paradise*, that explains what he has been through because of the corruption.

CD is the discoverer of the Chadam Protocol for curing cancer. Facebook page: Ambrosia peruviana for cancer.

A Bloody Nuisance

A Dull Night

Andrew Roland Betts walked along the sidewalk just above the high water line at the beach. The sun was setting. The colors were beautiful beyond description.

He'd read about the omens that such colors portended. While he didn't really believe in that kind of thing, he found they were accurate more often than not. That book, *Omen*, said that weird colors in the sky came true in most cases. The Indigenous people somewhere in South America depended on them.

Wait! That wasn't a true book, though the author used the reality of the natural things. His detective, Flint or Clint Somebody, was declared by the chief to be a member of the tribe or whatever.

Central America. Panamá. Clint Faraday.

What was this line of thought about? Where did it come from?

The colors. The fact he was to begin a new job, Head of Violent Crimes and Homicide, in about five and a half hours. The fact was there was almost no violent crime in Palmville, a ½-horse peaceful little town in the middle of nowhere.

You got promotions by solving big crimes in the police.

There weren't any to solve.

Well, Capt. Art, as Arthur Goins was called, understood that. He was a damned good administrator-type of cop. As good as they came. Curt Curtis, the only other cop on duty on the "Starter Shift" – 2:00 AM to 10:00 AM, was a good cop and smarter and quicker than anyone else he ever knew in the cop business.

Curt didn't want the violent crimes job, though he was in line for it. He liked to do the beat cop bit. He was a night person, so had requested he be on the "Blah" shift. It gave him time to read a lot and he knew every inch of the town and most of the people.

A sort of shadow crossed Andy's eyes, taking him a bit by surprised. He looked out to sea.

He actually had experienced one of those sunset flashes! The sky was a deep gold with small grey clouds, which wasn't too unusual, but the sea had been a deep burgundy color! It was just a flash, but was very clear. It didn't last more than three seconds, at most.

Now, if he were a native indigeno in Panamá, what would he read into that omen? The sky color was wealth and plenty with a lot of small patches of danger and sadness. That was easy. Gold and grey.

What about the sea? Burgundy? That wasn't red, so probably didn't mean blood. It was a rich, intriguing color that ... was that it? Intrigue?

It could mean blood mixed with something else.

Whatever, Andy suddenly wasn't nearly so positive that those omens didn't mean something. He had always been skeptical, but that flash was something seen by no more than one person in ten thousand or more in a lifetime.

He would become a believer if something happened to make it have meaning. Something unusual, rare and deep enough to give the moment meaning.

He went to a boy and girl standing by the low concrete rail in the park, watching the sunset.

"Did you see that?" Andy asked.

"See what?"
"Never mind."

Will Burke entered the Plum Pit Bar (Yech! That was a bar name?) to wave to the regulars there. He received a half-hearted response. He didn't have any friends there.

He didn't think he had any friends anywhere. He could feel he was tolerated, and that was the end of it. He couldn't decide whether he liked it that way or whether it was just convenient.

He ordered a cold one and took a stool at the end of the bar to sip the mug of so-so beer slowly. A woman, Irene Somebody, came to ask him for a light. He said he didn't smoke and didn't carry a lighter to help enable tobacco addicts. She knew that. She gave him the finger and went to Bob Sawyer, two stools away on the curve of the wide blue-tiled bar. Sawyer sighed and lit her cigarette for her, then told her to move away, please. Tobacco smoke gagged him.

Sandy Frenton came in, greeted everyone gaily, and was given the same reception Will got. He didn't acknowledge her, she ignored him.

Millie, the owner/barmaid, came to tell Irene not to bother the clients. Sandy sat on the other side of Sawyer. She ordered a short cold one and started a conversation.

Will could picture what that was like. The needy bit.

She had a little bookstore, mostly used, on the next block. The other "middle of town" street. Palmville couldn't exactly be called a city. It was stretching it to call it a town, but a lot seemed to go on there.

That was mostly because of the Walbert Research Center. Pharmaceuticals and development of new things to do with genetics and such. A patent on a medicine that was used for resistant fungal infections or some-thing. Will didn't think it was such a big deal. It was expensive and of limited use, yet it made enough to keep the company solvent? Harry Guest, part owner of the place and head accountant, said it cost about half a dollar to produce a tube of the crap that they sold wholesale for seven dollars and change.

Will asked if even that profit margin brought in that much.

Harry said it was international. One tube a day in every town or city of more than two thousand people was the baseline. That was on the order of sixteen thousand five hundred tubes a day. Profit of six bucks per. You figure it!

Will had a talent when it came to getting people to talk. Harry later said the company's records showed something a little different. For what the feds knew, they made three dollars per tube and sold about a thousand tubes per day. Don't spread it around, okay?

Will said he didn't blab. It was already obvious something was going on. Harry drove a Lexus, his wife drove a BMW, his daughter drove a Viper – for a company that was just able to hold its head above water?

Harry had slapped him on the back and bought him another beer.

Millie came by again to ask if he wanted another beer. He said he had to watch the budget.

"Oh? The job didn't happen?"

"Huh! It changed from a sure thing to 'Don't call us. We'll call you.' Typical."

She went on down the bar. Sawyer turned around to ask him if he'd talked to Wayne about the wiring job.

Will didn't have a clue what he was talking about, but said

he hadn't had time yet. Sawyer asked him that to be able to get away from Sandy. Sawyer talked a little about electrical wiring until Sandy moved away. Will grinned at Sawyer. Sawyer said, "Thanks. She can be one hell of a bloody nuisance."

They talked awhile about the research plant. Sawyer was the head electrician for the place.

"You going to the picnic at the lake day after tomorrow?" Sawyer asked.

"If I can."

He couldn't. Day after tomorrow, he was dead.

Sandy Frenton went into the Plum to see Will was there. She wished she could see from outside. She wouldn't go in if she knew he was there.

She sat next to Bob deliberately to distract him. She liked to irritate people like him. Her timing was good in that. Irene was standing there, with a cigarette, so he would already be aggravated by that.

Millie came to tell Irene to leave the customers alone. Sawyer chatted a minute, then turned to talk with Will. Paul Milton came in.

Yeah. right! Like he would have been having a conversation with Will Burke! Not if she wasn't there to make it the lesser of two evils.

She went to sit next to Opal Downs and Fred Haddon.

Opal was the private secretary to Mory Bertstein, CEO of Walbert, partner of Ed Walker. They had formed the partnership when Mory patented the formula for a fungicide that got rid of a lot of things that were hard to get rid of. Fred was production manager.

It seemed like half or better of Palmville were employed by Walbert.

Seemed like? It's the fact!

They talked about a lot of nothing gossip. She circulated for a couple of hours. Will left sometime earlier. She hadn't noticed. Other people came and went. Most of them, as she had noted to herself earlier, were employed by Walbert. There was going to be a company picnic to celebrate the patent of a new medicine of some sort day after tomorrow. She would be there to wander around, learning things.

It would amaze most people here to know what she'd learned by being a bit grinding and irritating. She played the needy bit to perfection. it was why she knew half of what she knew.

She would definitely be at that party! The company always supplied all kinds of free booze. People would do and say a lot of things they didn't remember ten minutes later.

Al Franks and Vinnie Vincent got into a loud argument just before midnight. That was the first time she actually noticed Will wasn't there. She automatically noticed where people were when there was trouble.

This was something about Vinnie's sister and Franks' brother. Al and Vinnie had never liked each other. That was probably a psychological reason the younger siblings couldn't stay away from each other. Harry and Bob broke it up. People were getting drunk enough that they would stop making sense soon. She decided to leave. She would see most of these and everybody else at the party.

She didn't make the party, either. Same reason as Will.

A Bloody Nuisance

A Bloody Mess

"Mornin', Andy. Welcome to the new job. Detective of Homicide or whatever. Probably a big deal almost anywhere but here. We haven't had a killing that wasn't solved in ten minutes here since the town was chartered. A guy gets pissed over a pool game and sticks somebody with fifteen or twenty witnesses or a husband or wife has all they could take and offs the spouse."

Capt. Arthur Goins was a good cop. He was a bit out of the time, but that didn't much matter in a place like Palmville. Sgt. Andy Betts was the new officer heading violent crimes.

"I can spend the time assisting burglary or whatever. Part of the job. Only thing that bugs me is that I have to be here at two in the morning.

"How come the captain of the ship is on deck at this ungodly hour?"

"Had to finish the quarterly. I keep putting things off, then end up doing all-nighters at the last minute. I keep promising I'll do it as I go, but never do."

"I'll set up a program on the computers. It'll all fill itself in anytime you need it. Push a few qwerty board keys and it's right there. Select 'print document' and you have the forms filled in and ready to be signed."

The radio came on. It was Officer Curt Curtis, the only other officer on duty this shift.

"Andy? Got one for you. Two. Alley back of The Plum Pit. One male, one female. Knife, and looks like torture, so it'll be heinous.

"Welcome to the violent crimes department, which Palmville never had any of until now! Your fault?"

"Know any reason?" Goins asked. "This is Art. I was here doing some paperwork."

"No. I knew both of them in a 'Good morning!' kind of way. They weren't popular, but were more nuisances than anything else. Maybe you'd like to smack them in the 'puss, but nothing serious.

"This is one sickening bloody damned mess here!"

"Anyone still at the bar?" Andy asked.

"No. Closed at one. Everyone gone by one thirty. I check it out every night. The bodies weren't here at one thirty, so they got offed ... maybe not. The lab we ain't got will tell us. I wouldn't have seen him then. The female ... what's her name? I know it. Shirley? Sandra! They called her Sandy. He's Bill or Will. Will the Pill. Donny called him that.

"I guess you'll have to get some kind of CSI crap going."

"I'll roust up Doc Blair," Art suggested. "He's as close to a ME as we have here. Andy's watched enough of that stuff on TV to be able to get by – and he's an academy graduate. I suppose. It's his case starting when this call was logged. Two sixteen.

"Instructions, Andy?"

"Don't touch or move anything. Keep anyone else from going closer than is necessary. Note anything about the area you feel might need attention. Notice anyone who just happens to walk by.

"In these kinds of things, I suppose you know you have to wear the latex gloves and shoe covers?"

"Ten four. Wearing. Got them in the glovecase. First time I ever thought of it, but that's why they call it a glovecase, right?

"I'm a little shook. The first time I see real dead murdered bodies is because I found them!"

"Secure the scene as well as you can. On my way stat!" Andy said. He saluted Art and headed for his car. He used his own because Palmville only had two cruisers. Curt was using one and Art would take the other home. The town would pay for gas and mileage.

"The lights go right across when you turn in. I saw what looked like a wad of rags. I might have seen it earlier, but didn't pay any attention. It's sort of behind the Dumpster. She's over there by the corner of the building. I didn't see her earlier, which could be because I didn't look and I was coming the other way. All I come through for is to be sure the door's locked and nobody's passed out or anything.

"Millie never misses that stuff, but I check, anyhow. I did catch that Jenkins character trying to jimmie the door that time and Irene Henson drunk and incoh trying to get in because she thought she left her keys inside when she had them in her purse.

"Whatever. I saw them this time!"

Dr. James Blair, GP, drove up and stopped. He had a younger girl with him he introduced as Anne Winters, intern. She was studying forensics, so he got her up and brought her along. She probably knew more than he did outside of hospital and office calls.

She was efficient! She started giving orders and railed at Curt for going to the bodies before forensics were there.

"How the hell else would I know if they were dead?" Curt snarled. "What? Stay twenty feet away and watch an injured victim die because *you're* still asleep somewhere? Hell-l-o-o-o-o!"

"With that much blood they weren't alive and you knew it!" she snarled back.

"My dear, you have no authority here. I've seen a lot more blood than that at an accident scene where the people *did* survive. The officer was just doing his duty. It's only on TV that the forensics officers – who are officially officers – can make demands and give orders. You are an intern medical practitioner who is studying forensics."

She turned with a snarling look on her face that instantly turned to embarrassed. She let a very small grin cross her face.

"Thanks, Doc. I do get carried away. You're right.

"Guys, when I get out of line, tell me. I won't get pissed, except for ten seconds. We have to work together."

"Well, Doc, we have to know the time of death as close as possible," Andy said. "Anne, was it? You say you won't get pissed.

"I see you're wearing latex gloves, as is Officer Curtis. Officer Curtis is also wearing latex shoe covers. You're not...?"

"Oh, shit! I deserve that! I'll guarantee hell will freeze over before I make that mistake again!" She used a digital thermometer, hooked up a little thing that looked like a cellular phone with computer access, waited a few seconds, then said, "Alive one hour fifty minutes ago. Dead one hour thirty eight minutes ago.

She went to check the female body. She soon announced, "Alive forty minutes ago. Dead twenty eight minutes ago. While I'm here, anyway, she was cut in no less than nine places I can see. The strong bruising around the mouth tells me she was muffled by a very strong person. She actually died of suffocation, but possibly from drowning in her own blood. I think more probably because the hand holding her mouth also covered the nose. There is no evidence of rape.

"Officer? Whoever did this has a *lot* of blood on him. He's powerful to have been able to hold her like that while she was struggling. She's not big, but she was in good shape and she's not petite.

"I talked to her a couple of times. She seemed introverted and shy, but that was personality traits. Physically, she was very damned capable. It seemed incongruous at the time.

"I'm not qualified. This is personal opinion.

"I think she was schizophrenic. Not pathogenically, but sort of ... maybe inherited or learned from a schizoid mother or something.

"I'm taking courses in advanced criminal psychology as part of the forensics thing.

"I want to be the first totally all-around CSI investigator. Seems I'm practicing all the things I know a little about this morning, eh what?"

"Yes. I saw that, but *had* a lot of blood on him," Andy replied. "Her purse is dumped right there. I would think that was post mortem. What-ever she was killed for is quite small.

"Process the purse as fast as you can. We need her identification and so forth from it."

"It's a fabric purse, so won't take prints except on the metal clasp. This wasn't done by someone who would fail to wear gloves." She dusted the clasp and used a blue light on the purse. "Nope. No prints or anything usable in or on the purse.

"There's also no identification in the purse. There's a key

pocket in the purse that's turned inside out. It would be hidden except for that. Something was taken from it. I don't think it was a key."

"Curt!" Andy shouted. "Do you know where she lived?"

"Who? Sandy?"

"Yes."

"Out on East Hibiscus. I know the general area."

"Get out there! Fast! Note anyone up and around. See if you can find where she lived. The killer might have her keys and is at her place."

"Roger!" Curt ran for the cruiser.

"With caution! Killer!" Andy yelled. Curt saluted and headed out.

"Doc? Will you check for ID and keys on the other victim? As fast as possible, please!" Doc nodded and went to Will's body. A minute later he said no keys, no ID.

Andy hung around, taking pictures of everything in the area with a digital camera, marking and tagging certain things for extra pictures at better angles. He stayed until Doc called for an ambulance and the bodies were being taken away, then headed back to the station. Curt called and said he found where Sandy lived and was outside. There was no one about in the area.

"Do you know where this Will character lived?" Andy asked.

"No. Out Baker somewhere, but there are ten or twelve side streets off Baker."

"I'll try to run it down ... no. I'll be there in fifteen minutes. We'll go through her apartment. We'll have to do the forensics bit ourselves."

"Roger."

Andy went to his desk to write a very short synopsis and to leave his used camera chip there, then headed for East Hibiscus. Curt was parked outside of a small cabin he said was Sandy's.

"I took the liberty of calling Donny Faulkner. He told me this was her place. Her name was Sandra Ann Frenton. She was a field agent for an agricultural supplies company out of Virginia. Jefferson and Lee Agri- Products Company. She had the book shop because she would go nutzo with a half hour of work and a fax a week."

"Really? Jefferson and Lee? Virginia? Maybe Richmond?"

"What?"

"I'd say she was on a witness protection program. If there was ever anything that sounds like the FBI, Jefferson and Lee from Richmond Virginia has to be it!"

"I guess. That means we do have a motive?"

"It means we *could* have a motive. We can't know and might never. I'm going to give it the try of a lifetime!

"Curt? What if that Will the Pill character is the same thing? Is the FBI putting a bunch of dangerous people here in Palmville to hide them?"

"You know something else, Andy? What if they're the ones who're supposed to be hiding someone else? That's why the torture? What if it's both?"

Andy looked thoughtful. "No. No way. Only one would be tortured if it was that.

"Curt, don't say anything to anyone about this conversation. Let's see who asks the wrong question at the wrong time."

Curt grinned. They went to the house. The door was unlocked.

"We're too late," Curt said. "If it was just someone, they

might have missed something. They had to be in a hurry. If nothing was missed, it tells us a lot about it."

"One look inside and we'll know which," Andy replied. "If there's a mess ... Curt, something isn't adding up again. Those killings were messy.

"Damn it! I think that's to be a warning to someone for something!"

"The FBI wouldn't be messy. If they weren't tortured, it would be FBI. They were, so it wouldn't be FBI. If this place is messy we're probably looking for a hired thug."

They went in. Nothing seemed out of place. The living room was, if anything, overly neat and clean, as was the kitchen and bath and second bedroom. The first bedroom was messy.

"Curt, this isn't searched messy. It's just messy," Andy said. "This is getting more and more confusing. Every part so far has things that point out that no one is what they appear, no clues are what they appear ... it doesn't make any damned sense!"

"It sure as hell doesn't to me!" Curt agreed.

"Can you call Donny? I need to know something."

Curt called Donny, who said he would never get his beauty sleep if this kept up.

"Donny, was Sandra a neat person or a messy person? This is Andy Betts."

"Betts? The hunk at the police? (Donny was gay.)(Oh? You figured that?) Sandra?

"Oh, right. Sandy. Curt asked about her. She's a neat freak. I don't think sh ... *was*?"

"She was murdered."

"Ayeee! What...? Oh, shit!"

"While we're at it, did you know Will the Pill?"

"Another past tense? Him too?"

"Uh-huh. Behind The Plum."

"Well, this has me ... sorta upset. His name is – was – Will Burke. He lives – lived – on Fern Drive, off Baker. He rented the little place in back at Aldriges.

"He wasn't really so bad. Neither was Sandy. They just didn't have a clue about personal relations, so people avoided them."

"Thanks, Donny. We'll go over there, but I think the killer will have beat us to that, too."

"We're going to Will's place?" Curt asked. Andy nodded. "After I get a forensics team in here to find what the searcher didn't."

"Except we ain't got no forensics team."

Andy grinned and took out his cell phone to call Dr. Blair. He chatted a minute. Doc said he'd send Anne and two hospital workers who were big enough to protect her if anyone came back. "How can you be so sure someone was there? Particularly, if he was, it was the killer?"

"Keys missing from her purse. Front door unlocked.," Andy replied. "Two plus two and that shit."

"That would be a telling point!"

It was twenty minutes later when Anne and two men came. Andy said the killer had searched at least that bedroom. He was professional. Any clues would be small things.

"Anne, there's something he was searching for. He might not have found it. He knows what it is. We don't.

"Get the idea?"

She nodded. "So. How do you figure he didn't find it?"

"His time was far too limited. He came here to start looking in the bedroom...."

"I see! He was interrupted by something! If he wasn't, there would be no messy room!

"What interrupted him?"

"A cop car pulled up in front."

Curt snapped his fingers and said, "Driven by yours truly. He didn't have time enough to search between when he killed her and when I got here, right?"

"It's the way I figure. Shall we head for Will the Pill's place?"

A Connection?

Andy and Curt arrived at Will's place to find the scene so normal and peaceful it could put them to sleep. While he could have been a neat person who had things replaced after search by a more normal person, he was no neat freak and no evidence he had been a messy person. The place was clean, but not obsessively so.

Andy stood in the middle of the kitchen after he and Curt spent two hours minutely going over the house. "This place was set up to be searched where whoever was searching would find zilch. So was Sandy's place," he said bitterly.

"That looked like the case at Sandy's to me," Curt replied. "Does the same thing seem obvious to you as to me? That we still don't have a clue as to which side they were on?"

"It occurs to me that Sandy was the one who set her place up to be searched, so that tells me where there may be clues. It also leaves the question of whether Will set this place up to be searched or if it was the searcher who left it where it would look like that.

"If there was anything here to find, it was found. That tells me ... that what was found ... that maybe Sandy was killed because of something from here.

"Damn it to hell! *What* is going on?

"Let's get back to ... no way! If there's something to be found, it won't be in that house that was set up purposely to be searched!

"Curt! Go sit outside of The Reader's Den! I don't think there's but one way out, so be where anyone inside can see you watching."

"I'll sit right outside the door." Curt went to the cruiser and left. Andy closed the cabin and put a crime scene tape across the door. That would make the killer wonder if he had found something there. Why else put up the tape?

He went directly to the station to use the connection with Judge Rauls to get a warrant for the bookstore. Rauls said to come pick it up. He heard about the murders and knew Frenton owned the shop.

He was heading for his car when he got a call. A man said there was someone breaking into Harold's Hardware. He said, "Ten minutes!"

He would check on that one. He radioed to Curt – as he got another call. He smirked to himself and told Curt to honk his horn in ten seconds. He answered to hear some guy yelling about someone with a gun outside his house!

There was the sound of a horn honking a little distance off.

"We've got you, turkey!" he said into the phone and hung up. The searcher was in that store with no way out but the front.

He warned Curt to stay where no one could get a shot at him. The killer was inside. The only way out was through him. Three minutes.

He raced to his car and spun out. There was one good thing about this being such a small town. He could almost run to the bookshop from the station in three minutes.

He pulled in behind Curt and went to talk with him a minute. He had the portable from the station with him and checked, but the caller to the office was private, which was the immediate thing he noted and why he expected the second call. Two officers, two cars. Set up two socalled violent crime scenarios and they would both be away long enough to escape.

"How will we get him out of there?" Curt asked. "He has the major advantage if we just go in after him."

"We let him see we'll outwait him. He'll soon get the message that we aren't in any hurry. We can literally starve him out."

Curt grinned. "What will he do?"

Andy shrugged and called loud enough for anyone near the front to hear, "Call the station number. I have the relay unit here!"

They waited. About a minute later the station phone rang.

"What's the deal? We have to starve you out or get SWAT or some-thing?" Andy asked.

"I'll come out. Don't get trigger happy. I didn't kill them. I'm looking for ... something to connect. I'm FBI."

"Come on out. You'll be covered from two places, so don't get stupid or you'll get dead."

A man in a dark suit came slowly out the door with his hands held in front of him. He was wearing latex gloves. He came over to them by the car.

"Now the other one," Andy said. "Don't play games."

"What makes you think there's anyone else? I'm Agent Manners," he answered innocently.

"I'm Andy. The FBI does not, ever, send one person on a dangerous assignment. If he was outside he would have already distracted Curt and you'd be gone. He's inside."

Manners laughed shortly and turned to wave at the door. He called, "Come on out, Sue!" He turned back to Andy and raised an eyebrow. A tall dark haired woman came from the shop. Manners introduced her a Agent Timmins

"Look, Andy. We can explain why we're here. We have to find what whoever killed them was looking for," Manners said. "They had some information that could get some people in really deep hot water."

"It's Officer Betts, Agent Manners," Andy answered. "No games. I read the book. Pull the big bad FBI agent act on me and you'll sit in the pen until some bigwig from WASH-ing-ton, Son! comes to get you out, then you'll still have the charges. The psychological crap can wait. I'm tired and I'm more than a little irritable."

Manners set his jaw and gave Andy a hard stare. He let a small sneer sit on his lips for a second.

Andy shrugged. "Sir and Madam, you are under arrest on a charge of illegal entry into a private edifice and with interference in a felony investigation. Anything you say will be taken in evidence and will be used against you in a court of law. You have the right to an attorney and all that, but you would reasonably know the Miranda, so I don't have to even say that much.

"You gonna get in the car or are we gonna put you in?"

"You can't arrest me! I'm FBI!"

"I just did. You gonna resist?"

Timmins reached to a pouch on her belt – and found herself staring up the barrel of Curt's Glock 90.

"Jesus Christ! I was just getting my ID! Christ!" she yelled.

"Uh-huh. I didn't ask for it. The two of you get in the car. Now!" Curt demanded.

Manners tensed and bunched his shoulders – and found that Andy also had a Glock 90.

"Get in the car," Andy hissed. "You just made a threatening motion toward a police officer who has placed you under arrest."

"I'm FBI!" Manners yelled.

"I have your word on that. I personally reacted to you because you made the claim but offered no proof. No more bullshit!"

Timmins sat in the car and said, "Come on, Gene. We'll handle this hotshit our own way. These two hick yokels will learn it's not smart to play the little tin soldier with the FBI. The hard way!"

"Now *you're* threatening a police officer?" Curt asked. "You really are acting in a measured intelligent manner (smirk), aren't you?"

Manners sat in the car. He let a giggle escape. Timmins asked what the hell that was about.

"We tried the act. It didn't play here, much less Peoria," Manners said. "Okay, Officer Betts. I'm Gene and she's Sue. I'm just getting my ID, okay?"

Andy nodded. Manners reached into an inner pocket and handed him a case with a badge. There was a card in the other pocket that said he was a special agent working for the Federal Bureau of Investigation.

"I'd say to take it out of the case, Sir, if I gave a damn," Andy said. "My father was a cop in Orlando. He had a murder case he was working on. The FBI came in and ordered him off the case. He refused, saying the murder was in an area where he was responsible for investigating and he would investigate. The FBI went over the captain's head and he was forced off the case. It turned out the killer was a man who worked for a foreign country. The FBI protected him. It led to my father getting shot. He was crippled for the rest of his life to where he couldn't work. The killer was deported back to his country, where he got a hero's welcome.

"I've studied the law. I know exactly how it works where the FBI is concerned. You can't interfere in my case without federal certification before a federal judge. You are to be treated just like anyone else unless and until you produce the certification. It's not retroactive. Any charges you incur before producing that certificate are under application.

"Are we clear on that point?"

"As clear as the finest crystal!"

"Okay. Now you can tell me generally what you're after. If I find it I'll share it with you or give it to you at my discretion."

"Gene!" Timmins cautioned.

"What the hell, Sue? They obviously know, so what difference does it make?" Manners replied, "They were special agents. There's something going on at that drug factory that's one hell of a long way from innocent research.

"We only know that because of people certain workers and manage-ment in the company meet with a wee bit too frequently and a tiny bit too surreptitiously – and the fact the company made a little more than a hundred grand last year, from which two directors bought a large estate near the lake ten miles from here and the two directing families spent something over six hundred grand on fancy cars, alone

"We were basically looking for the evidence they were anything more than private investigators. They carried that secondary identification to make it appear they were working on their own. We had placed a few hints that they were into petty blackmail.

"We have to know if the killer was hired or did it on his own. There's a little bit too much professionalism involved.

I was looking for ... any-thing to tell me if the department is known or suspected to be behind them. We want to get anything that would tie them to the department. We also want to find who's behind it and take care of that end.

"I suggest that we work together. I won't blame you if you refuse. Standard act four-B didn't work. Sorry."

Andy nodded. He said he'd work with them, that they probably knew a lot more than he did about searching.

"One thing has to be perfectly damned certain. One lie, one evasion, and you've broken the agreement. Either side. You or me."

Manners offered his hand. "Deal!"

"Then let's get at it. I'm tired."

They went into the shop. Curt and Andy split up and Manners and Timmins split up. They said what they were looking for – other than anything whatever that could help them – was a case like he carried. They had found the one at Bill's place. There was nothing else there that would interest Andy. That's all they took from the house except for some computer disks and memory sticks they hadn't looked at yet.

They were efficient. Curt found the badge case inside a wooden stair newel post figure. Manners found some papers hidden in the file cabinet that had nothing to do with running a bookstore. Andy found some other papers slid into books. Timmins found some papers hidden in books. There was a library card in one on the desk. Paul Milton. It wasn't a library book. It was a used book about trout fishing. Andy looked at the date record. Laine Bertstein? Never checked it back in and Paul Milton had it to return? That seemed odd.

Who the hell was ... maybe Mory Bertstein's wife or daughter? Wife. Daughter was Sylvia.

The sun was coming up as they finished. They went out, locked the place and headed for the station.

"I don't think we were noticed at the store. Someone may have seen the cars and thought it was you – which it was. You'd very naturally watch the place," Sue suggested. "How did you figure the papers were in books? More importantly, why those particular books?"

"The customers wouldn't look in those kinds of books. I've never seen anyone here who would be interested in very young children's books. They would also avoid the extreme religious works.

"The papers are in code? They seemed like the kinds of things people might have used as bookmarks or whatever."

"Yes," Manners answered. "How did you glom onto the fact that's not what they were?"

"Because the books would be checked before they were put on the shelves to be sure that kind of things weren't left in them," Curt replied. "I thought of that the first one I saw Andy take one out of. He listed the book and page number for each one in case that was part of the code."

"I think I'm gaining a good bit of respect for you local hick yokels!" Manners said. Andy and Curt both gave him the middle finger salute.

"That's local yokel hicks!" he corrected. "*Sgt.* Local Yokel Hick to you!"

That got *him* the fingers.

A Deeper Investigation

Andy sat back to think this one over. His training didn't leave him with much doubt that what they knew and suspected so far was close to what they would find.

He had taken photos of the papers they found. He downloaded them into the computer, moved all the evidence photos into a file with sub-files of which were for Sandy, which for Will, and which for both. He had a file for "other." He put the paper pics in that one.

He sat back again to think. Connections: the two were connected in that they were both FBI and that they were both investigating something about Walbert Pharmaceuticals.

That connected everyone who was in that bar last night, which was his next area to investigate.

The bar opened at 4:00. He would grab some sleep until then. It was now 9:38. He was on duty until 10:00. He could grab five hours. He would spend until 10:00 trying to decode those papers. They were about that plant and/or the people who worked there. Maybe about what the plant was producing.

Not that. What the plant was researching.

Manners had mentioned that the execs at the plant were meeting with suspicious people under suspicious circumstances. He would have to know who was meeting with whom.

He had his work cut out for him.

How trite!

"Hi, Millie! How's the bar business?" Andy greeted.

"Oh, hi, Andy. It was pretty fair until last night. You here about that?"

"Yeah. I need to know a few things about earlier."

"Let me get Sam to filling the coolers and we can talk. I don't think I know anything, but you never know. A barmaid sees and hears a lot that don't register at the time."

She went to the minimally retarded man who did the gofer and restock and whatever. They went into the big walk-in cooler in back and rolled out cases of chilled beer and a keg on a dolly. Sam hooked up the keg while Millie rolled the empty to the back and returned with another. She took an empty from the cooler under the bar and came back out to talk.

"We have the three kinds of draught, so that's handled. Sam can do the bar restock and put the beer in the coolers. You follow me around and we'll talk while I do the clean thing. I have to use the bacteria thing regular or the whole place stinks of stale beer.

"I can guess what you want, mostly.

"When they were here. Pill came in around sevenish. Sandy came in around fifteen minutes later. Pill left at eleven ten, because I note when anyone gets loud or fiesty. Al and Frank got into a yelling match about their sisters and brothers and so forth. Harry and Bob broke that up. That was eleven fifteen and Pill left five minutes before.

"You know I'm guessing at the time, but it will be five minutes one way or the other.

"Irene was cut off and sleeping at the table over in the corner." She pointed.

"Bob Sawyer was here when Pill came in. Opal and Fred

were down at that end of the bar. They went to that table (she pointed to the one just past the end of the bar). Sandy went to them after she talked with Bob for maybe five minutes. Bob talked to Pill and she moved.

"Bob usually didn't talk to Pill, but it was him or Sandy, and Sandy could be ... trying. She talked to Paul Milton when he came in about then. He seemed mad about something. She went on to sit with Opal and Fred.

"To tell the truth, her act was getting thin with everyone – and it *was* an act. She was actually a calculating, vicious, vengeful bitch!

"I'm saying all this in confidence, I hope!"

Andy grinned and nodded. "Unless you admit it was you who killed them."

She looked shocked, then grinned. "Oh, no problem! I would never admit it, even though it's exactly what happened. I snuck out while nobody was looking and shot them both, then snuck back in and acted like I was here all the time! Nobody even noticed I had blood all over me!"

They both laughed. "Ah-hah! Nobody said they were shot! I've got you!"

She grinned. "I don't know if they were shot or if it was the old blunt instrument or they were strangled. They were shot?"

"No. Cut up and maybe smothered, Sandy. Will about the same. You had to sneak out twice. They were killed quite some time apart."

"I don't know why I didn't see them when I closed up. They were where the tape ... I wouldn't look unless I had some crap to throw in the Dumpster, and that waits until the next morning. I guess I was just dead tired and thinking about the tax thing I have to pay today. I just went.

"Let's see. George came in and left after two beers. That John guy came in and sat at the end of the bar against the wall. He doesn't more than nod at anyone. Nancy and Frieda came in. They're lesbies. They know everyone and talked with everyone. They didn't leave until I closed. Bob and Harry and them.

"Jimmie Thomas and Donny came in for maybe fifteen minutes about nine. Jim Handsley came in and went after a few minutes. Carl Ober. Vinnie and Al, of course, Gilda Somebody – she's as much of a pro as we have here. She left with Daniel Kilton. He came in a few minutes before her, maybe ten thirty.

"It was a slow night. That's about it."

"You sold two kegs of beer to just them?"

"No. We had a good afternoon trade. Everyone was talking about the big party at the lake day after tomorrow."

"Okay. I have a general idea of..." He remembered the library card. Paul Milton was there. "... when everybody came and went.

"Oh! That Paul Mills. You didn't say when he left."

"Paul Mills? There was no ... you mean Paul Milton? I don't know when he left. He was there ... I saw him about twenty minutes after he said something to Sandy. I didn't see when he left."

They chatted a bit about things in general, then Andy went back to the station. It would probably come down to interviewing most of the ones at the bar. He still needed a motive. Without it, he didn't know where to look later.

He brought up the photos of the papers. He couldn't connect anything. It wasn't obvious. He could figure that the ones that looked like grocery lists had something to do with bars. 2 - 6 -

Millers could mean 2 sixpacks of Millers or could mean two people were at Millie's. 1 - Pabst could mean ... Millie's was the Plum Pit. This wasn't working.

It was time to go home. He nodded to Fannie Primton, at the desk, and went home.

Andy sat on the bench in the maintenance room until Bob Sawyer finished his instructions for wiring a circuit for an isolation chamber. He felt Sawyer would be the best one to talk to first. He had been talking with both Will and Sandy at the bar.

Sawyer came in to sit, looking expectantly at him.

"Mr. Sawyer, I need some information about last night. I tried to find you at the picnic, but they said you have a little emergency here," Andy said. "I'm Andy Betts, cop."

"I'm Bob, local asshole, if my wife can be believed, and she seldom can.

"The emergency was nonexistent. Much ado about bullshit.

"I'll probably go to the picnic later.

"What?"

"You were already there when either of them came into the bar. They both spoke awhile with you. I just need general information until I can determine what questions to ask. I won't try to make you think I know anything I don't know.

"Did either of them talk about anything that you felt might mean they were afraid of someone or something? Anything on that order?"

"Hmmft! Her, I couldn't tell you what she was whining about. I tuned her out before she sat down. Will, all he did was save me from her. I asked him about something. Tried to make it sound like he was looking for something for me. I think it had to do with specialty wiring or some-thing. It was make-talk.

"I mostly tuned him out, too. They were both a lot to ... I guess you'd say 'misfits' in the Plum. No social skills, to put it more or less like the headshrinkers might say."

Andy grinned. "How would you put it?"

"Classic pains in the ass."

"Seems to be the general consensus. Anybody you noticed talking to either of them or about them?"

"No. I didn't pay attention. I know Millie said something to her. She smirked the way she did when she got points up on someone. Paul talked to both of them, but he talks to all of us, regardless. He's what I'd call a natural-born mediator type. Harry may have talked to them. He would. Opal, because Sandy wet to sit with them. You could tell Fred didn't exactly get a big thrill out of that, but she couldn't see that people avoided her. She was blind about that.

"I sort of remember someone talking to Will just before he left. I'm not sure ... it may have been Paul ... or someone. It was someone you don't notice that much. One of the regulars who're always there or something.

"That's weird! I guess it's because I tried not to notice them. I don't know why I ... it was someone ... I can't even guess. Weird!"

"Where? On the floor? At the bar?"

"Hmm. It was at the end of the bar. His back was to me is probably why I can't think.... Maybe that guy who comes in and has one beer, doesn't speak to anyone, and leaves. John Somebody. It was down there where he always sat.

"Millie came up to them, but I don't think she even said anything. She was going out the walkthrough to collect glasses.

"It was right before he, Will, left. They both left, I guess. The next time I looked was when Will went out and I glanced over there. No one was there."

They chatted a few minutes. Andy said he'd go to the picnic. He could talk to everyone else there.

He was very thoughtful as he drove toward the lake. He was sure Bob had given him a clue about something – but what?

Irene Henson was waiting for a bus to go to the lake. Andy decided he'd give her a ride. She was probably too drunk last night to remember anything, but she might.

She didn't remember anything. She didn't even remember talking to Will or Bob or anyone else. She had been so tired after a long day she didn't remember much other than deciding to leave just before closing. She may have dozed at a table or something. She was so tired. Maybe she had a touch of flu or something that made her so tired..

Uh-huh. Flu labeled rye whiskey, Andy thought.

He pulled into the parking lot at the picnic meadow. Irene thanked him for the ride and headed for the big table with the free booze. He looked over the closer people, then headed down toward the dock where the waterski boat was running around the lake. Fred Haddon was skiing behind it at the moment.

Harry Guest came to welcome him and to offer a drink. He said he couldn't. He was on duty.

"Uh-oh! What have we done now?" Harry asked, aping shock.

"I don't think it was you. It's about last night and the murders. I'll try to be casual and discrete. I don't want to make a mess of the picnic.

"While you're here, anyway, did you notice anything about them last night? Who they talked with or anything?"

"They weren't the type I would notice. I think maybe she and him were talking to Bob. He would know if they were arguing with anyone or anything."

"I talked to him earlier. He doesn't know anything. He's like everyone else around here. They were both the kind of people you tuned out and tried to avoid."

"Yeah. They even knew enough about it to know the other one was somebody to avoid. They wouldn't even say Hi! to each other unless they were forced to. She had a talent for grinding on your nerves when he was around so you would go talk to him so she'd find somebody else to whine about.

"I sort of figure they were once a couple, but they broke up for some reason and she wouldn't let it go. There were a couple of times when he would grind on Opal's nerves and she would go talk to her to get away from him.

"What we called party-poopers centuries ago when I was a kid. Wet blankets.

"I think Fred talked to him a little, but that was because she plopped down at their table and he had to get away from her. Just a guess.

"Anything else? I'm sort of a greeter at these shindigs."

Andy saluted and moved on.

For people no one talked to, they didn't seem to have missed anyone last night!

That was their method. Get a guy pissed at him, he'd go talk to her to get away – and vice versa. They had it down to a science.

Millie was here? She walked by and smiled. He said he didn't think she'd leave the bar to come out to a picnic at the lake.

She laughed. "The bar opens at four. It's a quarter after ten. They buy the drinks from me. I give them a discount for volume."

"Logical!" Andy agreed. She went on over to the drink table. Opal was there. He would wait until later to talk with her. Dr. Blair and Anne were there. He talked with them for awhile and got the reports that stated pretty much that what they had was what they knew.

Sam, the big gofer at the bar, came to talk with Millie. He had spilled something all over himself. She sighed and rolled her eyes.

Andy was sure he knew something he wasn't aware he knew. Some-thing damned important.

Manners and Timmins were wandering around down by the dock, talking to Mory Bertstein. Andy grinned. The only two there in suits of any type, which made it seem like they were in uniform. He shook his head.

"They're some kind of cops? Working with you?

"I'm Donny Faulkner. I know who you are. This is Laine Bertstein, if you don't know."

He was with a rather attractive, but hard-looking woman. Andy smiled and took her hand.

"Well, I'll go mix and feel uncomfortable. If it wasn't for the fact these people work for my husband they wouldn't bother to speak to the damned Jew," Laine said. "You're new here. It won't be long before you learn how these ... *people* think of others. They resent that my husband is successful.

"I don't tink you're like that. You would have perhaps nodded very shortly, not taken my hand.

"I'll talk about the hair later, Donnie. Have fun! She walked off.

Andy raised an eyebrow. Donny said she was a Zionist type. She was a pain in the ass, but she paid very well for his advice. She thoinks everyone here charges her five times what they charge each other.

"Seeing she expects it, I won't disappoint her.

"I like Morey. Sylvia is okay, but she's a worse pain than Sandy and Will were , combined!

"Your friends? I won't say anything."

Andy grinned. "They're federal. FBI. I was just noting they look like they're in uniform. Not a good way to handle an investigation, in my opinion, but what does some local yokel hick flatfoot know about any-thing, anyhow?"

"You, I like. I'd like to know you better. Hmm?"

"Not my thing. Only on alternate Thursdays."

They laughed and joked awhile, then Andy went down toward the dock. Sue saw him and waved, so he went over to ask how things were going.

"As usual. They saw through us before we were out of the car."

"Well, you *are* in uniform. Nobody else is."

"Uniform? Oh! Too formal for a picnic, but it's all we brought."

"There's a Target and a Wal*Mart in Pricely, about four miles to the south."

"We don't care if we're known. It's easier than coming up with a story no one will believe anyhow.

"Have you learned anything?"

"I don't know. I have to talk with a couple more people, then go home and digest it. Nothing obvious."

"So we keep the beat. Gene's giving me the look to say we'd

better be going. If you want him to know anything, tell me. We don't want to be so chummy it interferes with what people will tell you.

"I don't have much to add to what we've already been over, except that Vinnie Vincent could stand a bit of a closer look. Our report says he's meeting with some people with a bit of dirt on their reps."

"Alvin Franks is pretty often seen with Lyle Turpin. Vincent is seen with Manny Lewis. I know. I checked it out a few weeks ago when I was on general detective duty. Curt knows them all. They're more local than I am.

"Turpin and Lewis use them. That means I can use them."

"You know somethin', Turkey? You surprise the hell out of me!

"See you later."

She and Gene got in their car and left. Opal was sitting on a bench under a big oak tree. Maybe she would know something. He started over to talk when Paul Milton came to sit beside her. They chatted until Fred came up from the lake, then went to the food table to grab some fried chicken and French fries to go with their garlic bread..

Andy was on duty, but the prohibition wasn't against food, and that food was damned good!

He talked with Ed Walker while he snacked – well, pigged out! Laine Bertstein talked to Paul Milton and Millie Seyers for a few minutes, then got in her fancy Mercedes and left. Andy unobtrusively watched as Mory saw her drive off and looked greatly relieved. Donny was passing by and saw it. "Well, she won't make a scene about anti-Semites, at least!" Andy gave him a thumbs up.

He didn't learn much. In his mind he was trying to connect

that code with these people – but wasn't sure the code referred to people, directly.

He was thinking when he went by the sandwich table. There was a book laying there. *Final Hunter*, by James Roland. Fred Haddon was standing nearby, talking with Carl Ober.

Could it be that? The base for the code?

He had written down which book and which paper. It was a slight chance, but it was a chance. The titles were obscure works, in most cases. Religious and children's books. There weren't many children in Palmville – and it was a long way from a religious town.

A Puzzle Solved

Robbin's Song by Annie Deran.
RS. He didn't have ... yes, he did! Robert Sawyer!
Mama's Baby by Elsie Vanders. That would be Mory Bertstein.
Mama and Sammy by Lilac Planter. That would be Millie Seyers.
Happy Goose by Helen Ford. Harry Guest.
Open Doors by Eric van Schmidt. Opal Downs.
Freedom Hall by Rev. Silas Moore. Fred Haddon.
Pride and Misery by Arlene Wahlberg. Paul Milton.
Edge of the Wall by Nancy Bride. Edwin Walker.
Joys of Freedom by Rev. Silas Moore. ?
Sad Paradise by Violet Flores. ?
Who was JF? He didn't have that one on his list.
Someone mentioned a John was at the bar. Bob mentioned him. "John Somebody."
He called Millie, who said the loner by the counter flap? Fields or Fellows or something. She called to someone, then said it was Feld. John Feld.
Andy thanked her and hung up.
Well, here was the list! He had a name for each paper found in a book. Except one. There had been nothing much on that slip. A question mark? Andy remembered something about a question mark and two dates on that page. Nothing else ... except *visit Mom on Sat.*
He needed to know what the code meant.
Didn't he?

This was his suspect list for the moment. Due to the strength of the killer he could eliminate ... Opal. That was all.

Okay. Opportunity. Mory Bertstein and Ed Walker weren't there.

Were they? If they drove up back there no one would see them.

Millie. She hadn't left the bar.

Harry Guest and Bob Sawyer hadn't left the bar. They were in sight the whole night.

Why wasn't Vinnie Vincent or Al Franks on the list?

Because they were inside when Will was killed, having an argument. Add to that they were already being surveilled. That was official and would be on the reports. No need to keep codes about them.

The argument could have been a deliberate distraction. If Will had yelled out there during the hubbub inside no one would have heard him.

John Feld did not work for Walbert. Bob would have known him if he did. It was even possible he had left with Will. Just before Will left he was seen talking with him at the end of the bar.

Except it wasn't anywhere near certain that he was the one Will was talking to. The person's back was to Sawyer

There was more missing than there was there. Something would have to be done to break the code.

Wouldn't she have that somewhere? Where? In what form?

He brought up the pictures of the papers. The first would be Edward Walker if he was right about what the book names meant. Two notes. One on page seven and one on page twenty four.

Remember eggs and milk. Call Mom after three. Call

brother about doctor bill. Pay on Tuesday. Therapy Tuesday afternoon 4:00.

It was on a torn piece of notepaper.

The second was, *Mom mean mood. Warn bro. Get DVD video for party.* That was on a pink StickEm.

Without some kind of translation it didn't mean anything to Andy, even he knew it was a code.

He sat back to consider. Maybe the only one who wasn't working for Walbert would give him a clue. He looked for the slip and brought it up. It looked almost like a check-out record. Just almost.

It was found on page 194. Near the end of the book.

It was just a list of dates. Every third day. The last date was a day before the murders. There were 83 dates. There was a small mark by each of them.

Andy called Manners to ask when Sandy started her job. About seven months ago.

"Okay. Who is John Feld? He with your bunch?"

"John Feld? I never heard ... wasn't he in the bar?"

"Uh-huh. She gave him reports every third day, I think."

"I'll try to track him down. I think, if he was the agency, he'd let me know before this."

They talked half a minute more, then Andy sighed and called Curt on the radio to ask if he knew anything about Feld. He didn't, but he would find where he was.

Andy sat to go over the notes quickly. "Mom" and "brother" were on a lot of them. If anyone had tumbled they would soon know that's what they were.

He thought for a minute, then went to walk around the area near the bookstore. He asked the merchants in the area about Feld. The barber three doors away said he came in every two weeks for a clip. He lived in the boarding house on Elm.

Andy went to the boarding house and asked if Feld was there. He was out back, reading. He read a lot and worked on electronic gadgets. He had fixed the cell phone for the manager.

A quick look. Feld was at a bench under the big Cedar tree, reading a book. Andy went to introduce himself. He said he was investigating the murders.

"Those two at the bar? Why would I know anything about that?"

"Sandy was giving you reports every third day. You were there earlier if not at the time of the first murder. You talked with him. Why would I *not* think you know a lot about it?"

A steel hard look flashed across Feld's face. He didn't say anything.

"What was going on? They were acting as double agents? You aren't the official one?"

He waited a moment longer, then Feld sighed. "I don't know who killed them. Sandra was only reporting to me about certain features of the research. My ... boss is interested in what is going on. That company is conducting secret experiments with genetic insertion that could be extremely dangerous to a lot of people in a lot of places. Your CIA is sponsoring it. It is not legal for them to be doing that research inside the boundaries of this country. This is but one of many such endeavors they sponsor.

"They are engineering a plague, we fear. It is to be a highly virulent and resistant form of *Pestis.*

"My orders are to tell you that and no more, should you arrest me."

"I wouldn't be surprised. I've heard hints that they develop that kind of thing because they can have a serum or cure if they're ever used."

"And you are so naive you believe that?"

"I believe most of the people working on those things believe it. No. I don't. There's no such thing as a plague being a defensive weapon."

"Our great fear is that it is as much as inevitable there will eventually be an accident. One of their plagues will escape their isolation chamber. It will result in thousands of horrible deaths. We wish to be able to warn people in this and other countries of what would happen."

"How would...?" Andy mused. "Would they kill them over something like that?"

"I don't think that is what happened. I have learned there is someone else involved, that truly enormous amounts of money are involved, that another country wants the results of those experiments, that they would then use their existence to blackmail virtually the whole world."

"James Bond, I ain't. It doesn't appeal to me."

"Nor to me. I merely interpret what I am told and offer recorded proof of some of it. I think it very possible it was discovered Sandra was recording things for us, thus she had to be eliminated. I supplied her with some very sophisticated surveillance technology. It is extremely sensitive and quite small. I imagine you found that."

"No. It explains why a key pocket was turned inside out.

"So you're brother and the DVD's were the times she gave you that kind of thing?"

"She had a book with dates she would deliver things. It was merely a note she left in a book at the bookstore. I would go there to browse. I received the material at those times. She was never seen talking with me. I always entered the shop when there were others present, so was able to appear to be a bookworm searching for collectibles or some-thing. I left her payments and equipment in the request box where people dropped notes for her to order special books for them. I would sometimes arrange where people saw me drop something in the box. Other times I would make as certain no one saw me doing so. It would seem suspicious if, every time I went in, I dropped anything there."

Andy nodded. "Who is 'Mom?' Is she someone being watched or will I find another person in this mess?"

"I have no idea to whom you refer. It is more likely she was someone to do with the Federal Bureau of Investigation. I am working alone here."

"Okay. What did you talk about at the bar? Could someone have overheard and struck out?"

"I didn't talk with him at the bar. I didn't talk to anyone at the bar, except to order another beer."

They chatted for a few minutes, then Andy headed back to the station. He wanted a serious talk with Manners and Timmins. He wasn't in the mood for anyone holding out on him. He thought that was plain from the first.

He would first go home and grab some sleep. He was still to go on duty at two.

He also wondered who was talking to Feld at the bar. He didn't seem to be lying. It wasn't Will ... and maybe it wasn't Feld? Maybe that association was just because Feld was usually on that stool. Who was talking to whom? Was it Will talking to ... who?

"You two made an agreement with Curt and me at the

bookstore. We agreed we wouldn't play schoolboy games." Andy came on duty and called Manners to demand he come to the station. "So why do I find Walbert is being investigated about deals to supply biological warfare methods for the CIA from another source?"

Manners stared open-mouthed at him. "You're shitting me! We're investigating because there was pretty good evidence they make one hell of a lot of methamphetamine and worse!

"What the hell..!?"

"Are you *serious*!" Sue cried.

"Yes. I think maybe we're about to get into some very deep and smelly shit here.

"Do you know who 'Mom' is in those notes?

"Incidentally, they were notes ... Christ! He only used the one book! How many ... you said you had let the word out they were into petty blackmail as a cover. What if they really were? What if they were ... no. Whoever killed them wanted some information about something. There wouldn't have been any torture if they didn't.

"Feld hinted there was some other country who wanted the research to use to blackmail the whole damned world.

"I told him I'm no James Bond. It doesn't appeal to me. I don't want to get messed up in some international intrigue case with some nutcases from the East or something. I can't handle that kind of shit! Damn it to HELL! What's going on?"

"I don't know, but I damned well intend to find out. If the agency's putting Sue and me in a position where we have to fight a bunch of mad scientists or something I'll ... probably do nothing. It wouldn't be smart. Not with the state of the politics that've infiltrated the agency.

"I resent the hell out of being put in something like this. It's a long way beyond the oaths I took. They gave oaths, too!

"Did you find both of them were in whatever the hell it was? I think Will wasn't involved in that, but there are things in Fenton's resumé that make me wonder.

"You know something? I think maybe Burke was tortured and killed for information he didn't have!"

Andy thought about it. Another place he wouldn't be at all surprised.

They talked and planned for awhile, then Manners and Timmins left. They seemed sincere. Gene and Sue were superb actors if they were able to fake shock and outrage as well as they did.

Andy had to find out who two people were. Mom and brother. He also had to learn how they were involved, on which side.

He called Manners back to tell him to search those memory sticks. There was something on the sticks that explained everything. Sandy, at least, used a code. She wrote what were probably only slightly attached notes to communicate. She didn't depend on memory. That meant she had it somewhere. They were, according to Sue, two four gig sticks and two eight gig sticks. You can put a whole library on one gig.

Andy didn't envy anyone the job of investigating those sticks. That would be days of reading a computer screen. Four people for who-knew-how-many days reading something three or four times the size of *War and Peace* looking for one name or association – and they might come up with zilch.

The more he thought about it, the more sure he was he was looking right at something that would tell him ... something.

There was that little dull nagging at the back of his consciousness that said he had an important answer, he just couldn't see it.

He turned on the percolator and went in the bathroom to SSS. He had some cold sticky buns in the 'Fridge and a box of corn flakes. And a banana to cut up in the cereal. And some raisins. And a thick slice of ham lunch meat.

He quickly fried an egg and heated the slice of lunch meat. A really good breakfast!

Well, it was after midnight, so it could be called breakfast.

He headed for the station. He noticed he was being followed. It would be damned hard to not notice, seeing he was in one of the two cars on the road at a quarter to two in the morning and the other turned every time he did. Hanging back half a block wasn't too effective for fooling anyone.

He thought of giving the follower the slip, but decided it wasn't worth the trouble. It was probably the CIA or FBI.

No. They knew better. They would put a tracer bug on his car some-where and wouldn't be anywhere he could spot them. They probably already had.

He called Curt, who was at the station checking in. He said he would be there in a minute. He wanted to know if anything had come up to discuss before Curt went on patrol.

Curt caught on that, seeing he would be there anyhow when Andy checked in, something was up where Andy suspected they were being monitored on the radio. He replied that he didn't have anything new or very important. Nothing new on Andy's case.

Andy parked in his regular spot and went into the back door of the station. The follower had stopped just around the corner on the other side of the station.

Andy quickly explained what was going on with the follower to Curt, who would find an excuse to stop them. Maybe they would find who was paying someone that amateurish to follow him. Maybe it would be one of the suspects. Curt saluted, grinned and headed for the cruiser. Andy went to his desk to go through what he had.

Not much.

He sighed, looked thoughtful, and sat back. There had to be a reason this happened now. It could be that someone discovered they were under investigation ... but why the torture, in that case?

He could come up with lots of possibilities, but there was a little detail that got in the way of each of them. The torture ... didn't fit anything other than to get information about Sandy, in Will's case.

Then Sandy wouldn't have been tortured.

Unless Will didn't have any information? Sandy was playing her own game he didn't know anything about?

That was the only way it even began to fit.

Okay. Will the Pill was only doing his job. Sandy had branched out on her own. That would fit if she was black-mailing someone. She had found something with the surveillance equipment Feld had given her that gave her ideas.

She should have known that the primary use of thugs and goons was to end the careers of blackmailers..

After half an hour of contemplation that was all he could come up with. He would investigate it from that angle – while never losing sight of the fact he could be dead wrong about it.

Curt called to say the follower was a Floyd Williams. He didn't have anything more to report about that. He told Williams he was an inch from being arrested for stalking, that

Amy Johns in the apartment in the next block had reported it. If he was found in the area again it would be enough to have his ass in a cell for investigation for three days!

He got back to thinking about his case. Curt would quietly investigate the follower. He was good at that.

Okay. She discovered a lot about the drug factory facet – only to find it wasn't about a drug factory, it was about an illegal biological warfare project.

Would the CIA order her killed her for that?

You gotta ask?

Those memory sticks should lead to who she was blackmailing and why.

Millie's bar was in the center of it all. They were there, the Walberts people were there. She was killed after closing hours. Her ID was... So! It wasn't her ID in that purse key pocket. Manners had her ID. There was a key in that purse, along with a miniature recorder..

He called Manners, who said it was one hell of an hour to call people.

"Gene, we have to find her safety deposit box. We have to hope we're first."

There was a pause. "You know about because?"

"You found her ID in the bookstore. She was blackmailing people. Where is the proof she had to have? Where is the money?"

There was another pause. "I'll get on it. I didn't go into those memory sticks except to see if she had a file that was marked, 'Clues in case I'm murdered.' I'm not the world's top-rated computer geek. She'll have everything on those things. It would fit her personality.

"I got her personnel and psychological records this

afternoon. She had been recommended for only very low sensitivity jobs because she had an avaricious streak and was corruptible."

Andy snorted. "So they put her on something they thought would be routine. It turned out to be something that was anything but."

"You didn't say, 'Typical!' I'd have to admit it."

Andy gave the phone the bird. Manners promised to get anything that even could be a safety deposit box location identification first thing in the morning. Offices opened at eight. He'd have it sent by eight fifteen and would bring it to the station.

The rest of the morning until Gene and Sue came in was boring. It was what a violence cop liked most of all. No reason for his job.

A Box of Trouble

"Here's anything the machines could find that could be what we need. We have to go through it." Sue announced, dropping a sheaf of several dozen pages on Andy's desk.

He looked over what was there. Numbers and dates attached to letters and what were rather obviously initials. Short squib-notes after each one, containing what could be phone numbers. One, on page two, stood out. It was just a little different from the others:

AOB – 9/2/8 – 894-30056.

None of the others was before 4/1/14. He pointed it out to Sue, who studied it, shrugged and passed it on to Gene.

"What makes you think this could be it?" Gene asked.

"Bank of America is three blocks down and one over," he answered. "If this is it, it will be number eight two nine or nine two eight."

"I looked for a box a couple of months ago at BOA," Sue said. "They have boxes from oh-oh-oh-one to one-oh-oh-oh. Hers will be oh-oh-five-six – if that's what this is."

Andy nodded. He called Judge Rauls and asked what he needed to get information about who had a safety deposit box.

"If you have the name and an information warrant or the box number and same."

"Box number. Possibly name," Andy replied.

"Living or recently deceased? If it's the latter I can expand the warrant to allow you to open it."

"It's the latter. Fenton, though she could have used a phony name."

"Hm. Number?"

"Oh-oh-five-six or oh-oh-six-five."

"Okay. Ten minutes. Bank?"

"BOA."

"Yeah! Chinese bank named Bank of America."

Andy, Gene and Sue went over to the courthouse, got the warrant and headed for the bank. They went through the rigamarole of flat refusals until Gene called someone who spoke for a minute. The super-efficient bureaucrat running the section didn't say anything. She got out a ledger and said, "Oh-oh-five six is Frank Jamison. Six-five is Sally Fellows. We don't have a Sandra Fenton."

"How do we contact Fellows to be sure she's the dead body we want to get into that box about?" Sue asked.

The woman, Gladys Keller, looked up an emergency phone number. It was Sandy's. "You can use the phone on the desk."

Andy showed her the number on the police report. "It's her. She's dead. Murdered. We have to get into that box."

"Oh, dear! That woman sliced to pieces behind that bar?"

"Not that bad, but it was a bloody mess."

"You have to have her key. We have ours here and she has to use hers at the same time. Oh, dear!"

"The key was removed from the body. We believe it's why she was killed. What's inside that box can name her killer for us," Gene said.

Gladys went to a small safe embedded into the wall, opened it with a key and combination, found the key, and went to 0065. She inserted the key and said for them to place their key.

"We don't have the key. The killer took it. I can use a Sesame, which isn't available to anyone outside the agency,"

Sue said.

"These are designed where those things won't work," Gladys sniffed.

Sue grinned, took a small box with little wire-like protrusions, said, "It was a six-ridge key." She inserted six of the thin projections and set a tension spring, then wobbled the device back and forth for about fifteen seconds. It turned. She reached to turn the bank key and slid the 4 X 6 X 18 inch box out to sit it on the table.

"We need a second camera, I think," Gene said. He was recording everything they did on his own.

Andy said, "Right back!" went to his car for the police video camera and returned. They opened the box with Gene taking the overall scene and Andy focusing on the box.

"Well, here goes! Pandora's box! A box of trouble for someone!" Sue announced. She slid back the top and flipped it open.

"Probably for several someones," Andy added.

Sue took out two gold bars. They were stamped. Ten ounces apiece.

"First discovery; two ten ounce gold bars. Value will be something over thirty thousand US dollars. Next, what appears to be a very good diamond pendant. I'd estimate about eight carats. Three fifty-packets of hundred dollar bills. Another thirty thousand.

"An envelope of perhaps twenty photographs. They appear to be the type printed from a digital camera. They are of, usually, two people each. Some have three. There is writing on the reverse in marker. They will be examined at the lab."

She put the photos back into the envelope.

"There are three diaries. They seem to be records of dates

and places and persons. There is text covering part of each page. These will also be examined at the labs.

"I recall there was a like number on each of the reverse sides of the photographs, one, two or three. I theorize those numbers refer to the diaries.

"That is ... there is a small ... envelope containing what appear to be color film negatives. Individual pictures. Thirty five millimeter.

"That is all. We will place it into evidence bags and transport it to the offices. We request that Officer Andrew Betts accompany us at all times until this evidence is safely in the hands of the agency experts."

They had all, except Gladys, been wearing latex gloves since they entered the vault. Sue carefully sealed the evidence bags. They put them into a cardboard box Gladys found and headed for the station.

"This could prove very interesting – if you go for understatement," Gene suggested. Sue and Andy gave him the finger.

Andy and Gene set the videocams to be absolutely certain nothing would be missed. Anything hidden from one camera would be in view in the second. They adjusted the sensitive microphones on each, then Sue took out the packet of photographs.

"We will identify as many of the subjects as we can on these photo-graphs after placing each individual photograph into a clear envelope. I will now place the photographs into individual envelopes and mark each with a code number. The code for this case is PV one slash two.

"This is PV one slash two slash one. ... .PV one slash two slash twenty two."

She had the 22 photos lined along the desktop

Gene took over: "This is photo code one. It is of two people. There is what appears to be a briefcase that is open on a table between the subjects. It appears there is money in the case. It is not clear enough at this unmagnified size to determine with certainty. That will be a job for the lab.

"There is the number 'two' and four hyphen twelve hyphen fourteen. I assume the date the picture was taken. To be determined positively later.

"The subjects are, number one on the left, an unknown male. The subject two is a man identified tentatively as Harold "Harry" Guest, an employee of Walbert Research.

"Next, we have ... ... thirty four persons, many of whom are repeats. There are eleven persons we recognize definitely; Harold Guest, Mildred Seyers, Phillip Milton, Frederick Haddon, Robert Sawyer, Mortimer Bertstein, Edwin Walker, Samuel Price, Johnathon Feld, George Harris, and Nancy Lister. There is a strong possibility we have identified Carl Ober and Daniel Kilton as others, but they are uncertain. That leaves twenty one to identify. One is a man who seems very familiar, but no one here can place him. He appears in two photographs, one of which is with Mildred Seyers."

"Sam! Sam Price. He's the clean-up man at the bar. Retarded, but not much. Big enough that the drunks don't go too far. He could toss them out from the other side of the room," Curt said, looking at the photo.

"A police officer at this precinct has just arrived, Curtis Curtis. He says he may have additional information about several others in these photographs as to identification. His words, as recorded here, state that they are probably mob connected, due to the places they were observed and the persons with whom they were known to be connected.

"It is theorized among us, as also recorded, that there is some kind of conspiracy which, when added to what we might have determined about Walbert Research, implicates very powerful and dangerous people in a scheme we can only speculate as to purpose.

"Officer Betts?"

"We aren't equipped to further study this evidence. It is to be placed into the hands of agents of the FBI who are just now parking in the lot of the station. I ask that this department be carefully informed of any matter that will or can affect the safety of the people of this town."

Gene and Curt put everything into a cardboard evidence box and sealed it carefully. Curt took the box to place it on the table in view of the camera after a trip to the evidence room with it to add the seal that couldn't be tampered with.

Two men came into the office, showed some identification that Gene looked at cursorily and that Andy glanced over, but he knew it could be phony and he wouldn't know it.

They were filmed taking the box to their car and locking it into the trunk. They saluted and drove away. Everyone went back inside.

Curt caught Andy's eye and grinned. He chuckled, then laughed.

"What's the joke?" Sue asked.

"Those two. They were as much FBI as my dog."

"WHAT?!" From Sue and Gene, alike.

"Oh, come on! Two strangers to pick up sensitive evidence, and in a passenger car? Would the FBI, as screwed up as they are sometimes, do something like that? I suppose the real agents will be here any minute. We have good pictures of those two and their car. I got the license plate. I'll run it, but it will be for someone who had a plate stolen.

"I've seen that big black one around Young's Billiards. He's a punk hood."

"But..!!" Sue cried. "They have the evidence!"

"No. Curt exchanged the boxes when he put the seal on them." Andy said. "What do they have, Curt?"

"The wastepaper basket crud from the front desk and a brick."

An armored truck pulled into the lot. A man and woman came in, the woman carrying a Uzi. She greeted Sue and asked what they had for them.

"Hi, Amy. Some stuff that could put some biggies in the pen."

Curt got the real evidence box. Roger Phelps, the other FBI agent, signed for the box with his fingerprint over the signature. He and Amy left.

"You want a job as an agent? A department head job?"Gene asked Curt. "You could get it in a heartbeat for that!"

"Not in this lifetime," Curt replied. "Here's the data on the license plate. Winifred Ethel Himes, eighteen twelve Orangeblossom Street. sixty four years old. Glasses required to drive. Ninety nine Honda Accord.

"I guess she disguised it as a twenty thirteen Mitsubishi. They would never guess she's a secret FBI agent. Winnie sure fooled me with her disguise! A hundred ten pound five four white woman disguised as a two hundred pound six two black man!"

"We have two people to pick up for impersonating officers and evidence tampering," Sue suggested. "Maybe they'll tell us a few things to avoid spending the next four to six in fed!"

A Bloody Nuisance

A Comparative Listing

Andy took his copy of the videos at the bank to his desk and ran the memory to his personal comp. He had been careful to get every page in the Diaries on the video while appearing to be simply flipping through to see if there was anything slid in between the pages. The bookstore gave him plenty of reason to think there might be something there – though he knew there wouldn't be.

Three hours. It still was either plain as day. Blackmail payments.

Or too obscure for him. Coded evidence.

He went back through to see what changed from the first to the last in what was listed.

The notations were made with different pens. Some blue and some black. There were a few in pencil. A couple were red ballpoint.

That would be logical. She made the notes with whatever was handy.

He decided, seeing he didn't know what was important and what was not, to list the different coded with what was used to input them.

Avb, Bva, Vab, Bav, Vba, if he was right about how it was done, were the same person. Three letters in any combination. He noted that the code was in blue ballpoint until about a quarter of the way through the diary, then was in black.

Fde, Fed, etc. Pencil for two, then blue for the rest.

Mlk, etc. pencil for one, blue for three, then black.

All pencil notations were the first and first and second for all of them in all three diaries. He would theorize that was the suspicious phase.

Then blue ink. She found proof or whatever.

Black ink, she was collecting blackmail or something.

In diary two, Jop started with one pencil, three blue, nine black, and the last, red. It was about half the pages filled out in the diary when that last appeared. What did that mean?

He sat back to study only the three letter ID codes. He wondered if they were initials of some sort.

Robert Sawyer. What was his middle name?

He looked it up. Arnold. There was no Ras.

There was a QAR. That could be R-1 true middle S-1

Mas. Mildred Anne Seyers would be Lar. That was there. Okay. Jop.

Shit! He didn't have the order to work from!

He noted the date on the red note. 6/4 Lnsdl.

Lnsdl? There were other notes with that after the date. Not many.

He went back to the notes with that. One had 5/10 Lnsdl-Geo-CK.

Landsdale! June ten! Oel met with Jop at the Chicken King!

Well, two people he couldn't yet identify met at the Chicken King Restaurante in Landsdale, thirty miles away on June ten.

It was now important to know exactly who those two were. Damned important!

Backtrace. Red could have a psychological meaning. There were only three and they were the last with those ID codes. That could mean exit subject.

He used the police net to ask what had happened, who died, apart from not-natural causes, on June fourth.

Earl D. Druench and Isaac O. Quarz were drowned in a

freak boating accident on Lake Emerald.

Jop = Isaac O. Quarz.

He asked for full information on both victims.

Earl Daniel Druench was a PI with a shady reputation. The sleazy divorce lawyer type who took on cases for people like (suspected) drug suppliers such as Mannie Lewis. He was partner with a Floyd Williams in an agency.

Floyd Williams? The follower? That would definitely take some investigation!

Isaac Oscar Quarz, immigrant from Europe. Little known about him. Never in any trouble that was reported.

Fenton had something strong on him. She was investigating Walbert Research. They were suspected of running a drug factory. He was killed in company with a drug dealer's PI.

It almost added up. If they had been executed, that's what it would be.

They weren't. It wasn't that.

What would it hurt for him to go into fantasy land here? He was looking for clues, as Joe Walsh sang, "At the scene of the crime."

(1) Fenton was investigating Walbert for the FBI, trying to find proof Walbert was producing drugs.

(2) Druench was following Quarz for ... not Lewis. Who?

(3) Fenton found something that didn't have anything to do with the drug trade. It had something to do with international consequences.

(4) Ouarz was a sleeper. An agent for another country ... so he was a contact man for a foreign country. Fenton learned that when he met with Oel in Landsdale – so Oel is a foreign middleman contact. That meeting fingered Quarz and Druench.

How?

A fuck-up! Oel was who hired Druench, Quarz was stupid enough to tell Geo he was being blackmailed. Druench and Quarz were now a deadly danger to Oel – and so was Fenton. Fenton was investigating Geo, who didn't know it until that moment. Quarz and/or Druench had led to the finding about the whole scheme.

Exit Quarz, Druench, Fenton, and by mistake, Burke.

Burke, as Andy suspected, was tortured and killed for information he didn't have. He was never part of any of that end of the deal.

P-e-M: M-e-P.

Paul Evan Milton.

He wasn't the foreign contact. Quarz was the middle man between him and the contact.

Was Floyd Williams working for Milton or the contact? Or both? He would be the sleazy type to work both ends.

Milton did *not* kill Burke, but he might have killed Fenton.

It was a matter of elimination again. It was not Milton talking with Burke at the end of the bar.

Who could it have been? Who could manage ... obvious! It was the man upon the stairs who wasn't there, only he was there and not seen! He was always there and was seldom seen!

Seldom noticed. He was seen by all of them. Like the tables and chairs and booze behind the bar, he was seen only when he was the specific focus.

Sam Price. He wouldn't be noticed if he walked out of the place with Burke. Nobody noticed when Burke left because he was with Price, who was a background figure nobody noticed consciously.

And Sam Price could be used. By only one person.

Did Paul report to Millie or *vice versa*? It had to be. Nothing else fit the whole thing.

There were a lot of people who knew what was going on, they each had a part in it meaning they wouldn't blab. They wouldn't do anything to give away their part or anything about the scheme. It was their way to millions and to power they could only dream of.

Andy remembered same little facts about their lists. He figured they were back-up insurance. She could tell them they might get the safety deposit box, but there was another place the evidence was stored they wouldn't get. It left her two ways to go in all instances.

That meant he had to decode the lists.

What? he was out of his mother-loving mind?! Get more involved in this kind of shit?!

Be honest. He didn't have anything to do in this job. Less that a week ago he was complaining that it was boring. This kind of thing simply couldn't be happening in a place like Palmville!

He wanted every list that mentioned "Mom." He wanted to know just how deep Millie was into this.

He took out his copies f the notes. He had something to go on. It was a matter of finding what that was.

He would talk with Ed walker and Mory Bertstein. He could claim that there was evidence that Fenton was blackmailing some people at the plant. See what their reactions were to that one! It could tell him a lot!

A Bloody Nuisance

A Couple of Interviews

"Mory, we've known each other for a little more than a year to say good morning to. I'm Andy Betts, police investigator and all that crap. This is the first time I've had to meet you with departmental reasons.

"This is Curt. I think you know him better than you know me."

"Yes, Andy. Terrible thing. Who would have thought we wold ever have mutilation murders in Palmville? It scares the hell out of me! I have a wife and daughter!"

"Mory, the woman, Fenton, seems to have been black-mailing people. That led to her getting killed. People thought Burke was part of that, but he wasn't. He was FBI," Curt said.

"I was told they both were."

"Well, let's just say he was legitimate. She was working another plan altogether," Andy replied. "Him, we'll go after the killer with every-thing we've got. Her? I can say the priority is less. A lot of people get killed because they got into blackmail. They never learn."

"Andy, I know you can't tell me this, but is that Manners fellow FBI?"

"They have a reputation for not letting that kind of information out," he answered. He wouldn't lie about it, but that didn't mean he would tell anyone anything. "I find several cheap PI's are in it. One was killed, along with an agent for a foreign country, in Landsdale." Mory was suddenly a bit too casual, but he was also suddenly sweating. That one was a bullseye!

"Er, uh, I suppose. I don't think any local PI would be involved in with the FBI, you see. They don't work that way – or so I'm told."

"They don't work *with* anyone!" Curt declared. He could see what Andy was doing. "I think FBI would march in with the big bad govern-ment agent line and start giving orders with a case they were involved in. I haven't had much contact with them that wasn't that way."

"Which I would ignore. I know about FBI," Andy said with a grin. "I would see if I thought they could help me before I would agree to anything with them."

"Those two, Manners and that woman, were at my picnic. Wearing cheap shoes and business clothes and trying to blend in. It was funny. They could have been wearing those orange FBI vests and wouldn't have been so conspicuous!"

"Be careful, Mory. Maybe that was what someone wants you to think. Maybe someone wants to try to scare someone for some reason.," Curt suggested."

"Yeah. It did seem a bit over the edge, didn't it? Never thought of it. Could be.

"Andy, why are you telling me this?"

Andy pointed to the hall door and motioned to go out. Mory looked shocked. Curt looked confused. "I have two people who have been murdered. The difference between them and everybody else is that they didn't work for Walbert Research. That's sort of weird in a town that is, basically, an employee settlement." He motioned more urgently for Mory to go. Mory stood and looked questioning. He said, "Well, I have an appointment now. Could you come back in an hour or so?"

Andy motioned for Curt to go out. He stood and said, "We can come back tomorrow, I suppose." He motioned for Mory to follow as he and Curt went out. He pointed to his ear and raised an eyebrow at Mory. Mory nodded very slightly and managed to run his finger in a circle around the room. "I'll walk you to your car. Maybe you can tell me what Landsdale has to do with me."

"It's just an odd. kind of thing that.." Andy replied as they went out. They were by Andy's car before they spoke again. Andy said they probably couldn't be overheard there, but don't move the lips much as they spoke and keep looking around. He said he spotted a tiny wire where there shouldn't be one in the office. Mory said he thought it was bugged. What was he really there for?

"Because something is going on, and it's ... sinister. There are some dangerous people coming here. I don't know why. I don't know who they are or who they represent. Because there are some good people here.

"Mory, are you in over your head now? Did you just think you had control?"

Curt was looking at him like he was totally insane.

"Oh, dear God! They said I would make actual billions and no one would ever know anything about it! Paul gave me a million dollars in cash. It's some deal with some place that wants a kind of bacteria spliced that will produce something like botulism, only three times as strong. They claim it would be used to make antitoxin for this country, but that concentration would counteract any possible antitoxin, not to mention it wouldn't be any good unless you were right there before the body had absorbed any of it.

"I would never give them anything like that if I did make it! They claim to be the CIA, but I don't believe it! Oh, dear God!"

"I believe it," Curt said sourly. "They do things like that. If you finger them, you're dead. We do have mad scientists or military monsters who are running things like that. It's what the world is anymore.

"I don't think they should ever get any of that kind of thing, but we should stop what we can."

"I never had any control," Mory said bitterly. "My lovely wife sold me out. She wants Sylvia to be a billionaire. She uses the excuse that nobody likes us because we're Jewish. She and that Millie woman who has the bar. Nobody knows Millie is Jewish, but nobody seems to think anything about it with me and Sylvie says, 'Nobody,' as the young say nowdays, 'gives a flying fucking shit if you're a Jew or German anymore. Big fucking deal!' It's only the stupid radicals on this side and the rednecks on that. We don't have either here.

"I checked. Did you know Millie was financed into that bar by a Russian group who were once KBG? The Sam character is her body-guard or whatever you call them. I think he takes orders from someone else.

"Dear God! I wish I'd never heard of botulism or gene inserts!"

"Oh, she's found a really extreme radical for this place. Her!" Andy replied. "I agree with Sylvia. Who the hell gives a fucking flying shit? You aren't responsible for your ancestors' idiocies and neither is anybody else. Welcome to the twentieth century!"

"If we could only get through to both sides in the East," he answered, sighing. "Andy, I've only talked with you a couple of times, but I've always liked you.

"So long as the situation was just a bunch of half-baked Neanderhals sniping at each other and trying to be king of the mountain, it only amused me. It got scary when I realized it is no silly juvenile game those people are playing. They actually think like that! I have to find a way out! I have to!

"Andy, people being hurt or even killed is a long way too far. A very long way. I can't live with knowing I'm involved in it.

"I'm not the stereotypical whiner. It *is* my fault! I didn't have the spine to tell them to take a flying leap. I went along with it. I knew it was crooked, but not in what way."

"I saw that in you. I saw the way you reacted in the office..

"Mory, this is a dangerous situation in a lot of ways. I don't think I've ever known of anything that brings personal danger to myself and a lot of people I'm responsible for protecting to nearly this degree. I'm far too short of solid information. I don't want to increase the danger. Not when it can result in deaths.

"I think you've given me a bit of a direction.

"The safest thing I can see is to let them think I'm going down a side path somewhere, that I think it's about drug dealers in Landsdale that Fenton was blackmailing.

"Mory, and you, Curt. Spread that we found two papers in Fenton's things that I can tie to Turpin and Lewis and a drug dealer in Miami. I think that really is there. Let them think I can tag them and finish this case. Don't hint that I know about the FBI or anything else.

"Understand?"

Curt grinned. Mory nodded seriously.

They chatted for a bit more. Andy felt they were being observed, so he showed Mory a couple of sheets that were just laying there on the car seat. Mory would say he showed a paper he said was a code that he could only break in a few cases, but that very definitely would put Turpin and Maybe Lewis in the pen for twenty to life without.

Mory went back inside, Andy spoke for a few minutes with Curt. Curt would let it slip in certain places that Turpin and Lewis were in for some surprises and had better get their affairs together. They wouldn't be around for the next twenty, at least! Some guy by the name of Marianas in Colombia was about to fall and take a big crowd with him.

Marianas was a name Curt heard several times in a way that made it clear he was big in the cartels. There were four or more in the family, so they wouldn't be sure which ones – but Turpin and Lewis would. Turpin was working with one cousin and Lewis with another.

Now to do what he should have already done, but it hadn't come up.

Until now.

He went to the station, pulled the computer around, and input Mildred Anne Seyers.

Father William Alan Seyers, Swiss nat. USA, mother Sarah Lillith Solomon, USA.

Paul Milton was from Wisconsin. He attended college in Colorado. He was an average student. Business management major. Specialist in import/export law. Worked for an international company that supplied medicinal agricultural products for nineteen years before moving to Palmville.

Samuel Price was from Oregon. He never finished high school. IQ about 86. Worked for Seyers since she opened the bar. No information between.

Edwin Walker was born in North Carolina, spent his youth in West Virginia, moved to Georgia. Finished masters degree in General Family Medicine, then took advanced genetic courses. Graduated with minor honors. Wife Roberta nee Cline. Little known.

Who else?

There was a connection. It was through Millie or Paul. One of them was a deadly danger to the other, which made them deadly dangers to each other. Maybe the diversion of Turpin and Lewis would keep that on the back burner.

All of this hung together very shakily unless he could connect the missing link – at least, if he could find who *was* the missing link.

What brought it to such a head Fenton and Burke had to be disposed of? Burke was by mistake, but whoever connected didn't know they were working at cross purposes. That seemed clear enough.

But! Now they did! They would know they'd made the big mistake.

Andy didn't doubt Sam Price was the killer. He didn't know who gave the order. He had to know if it was an order given because an order was received.. If it was received, Millie acted on it. It had to come from Paul, but that made no sense.

It could have come through Paul. It wasn't from Mory Bertstein. That left Edwin Walker.

If he was in charge.

Laina? Would she be that involved and that ... yes. That would mean the order came from the Zionist Movement. It would explain why a Zionist would stay married to a mild person like Mory.

The FBI was working without knowledge of the facts behind the case already. Was someone else working with as little information?

Yes. There was a good chance that was the case. Someone

working from a false set of facts. Someone who was working for the ones he was supposed to be exposing. Only one here fit that.

Was it even possible to protect Feld?

Andy called Curt. They chatted a few minutes. Curt would try to keep an eye on Feld if things heated up.

Could Andy do anything more until someone else reacted? He didn't think so. He had to stop a murder, now, or several. He was unequipped to deal with what was, apparently, some kind of international intrigue.

He was lucky. There wasn't the stereotype-reaction here that was in nearby places like Landsdale. There, there were a lot of anti-Semitic ideas.

How stupid! Very few Jews nowadays were of actual Semitic stock people. They were Caucasians. There were only a small percent who were the hard-line radical types.

Feld, Seyers, Milton. They were the logical next victims, each for a different reason that was the same reason. Have the real heads of this hidden. Do not allow exposure of the actual slime doing this kind of thing.

It was to the point that Andy had to know the entire truth of the FBI's involvement.

Not true. They were involved all the way. It was a matter of if they were going to play their games and leave him in an impossible position to protect some slimy monster spy or something somewhere else. That was what happened with his father. It was *not* going to happen with him.

He finished his shift and went home. He was going to sack out enough to keep going, then he was going to find a little information about some people. The more he thought about it, the more sure he was that he and Curt were on their own.

Maybe he and Curt and one other. Something occurred to Andy then. He smirked slightly.

He almost didn't catch that one. Everyone already knew they were working together. Why try to hide it?

Because there was another worm in that apple?

He concentrated on everything that happened when both the FBI and Andy were concerned. And Curt.

Andy got up at 4:30, cleaned up, and went to Lily's Restaurant for a good dinner – for a change. He chatted a bit with Lily to learn some of what people were saying. The drug thing was circulating just under the surface. Maybe it wouldn't go all the way to hell before he learned what he had to know.

He called Curt, who had Kyle Herndon tailing Feld. Kyle was a good man for the job. He was keeping Milton under surveillance and Fannie was keeping a discrete eye on Millie's place. Everything was calm enough for the moment.

He called Manners. Timmins was somewhere watching Walker, he had been watching the plant. Everybody else was there. It was almost time to go home.

He thought, then walked out toward the plant. It was a half hour's walk, but he didn't want anyone to suspect he was going there. He wanted to see exactly where one person was.

He stayed on the side street where he could see people leaving the plant. Everything seemed normal.

Walker's car was there when everyone else was gone. Bertstein's car was there, as was his wife's. There was a car, a grey Honda, near the entrance, but outside the security fence. He recognized it. He managed to get close but to stay out of sight. Manners was sitting in the car.

He was about to go slip into the car when Fannie came out of the plant, looking around for someone, went back inside, and came out again four minutes later.

What was she doing at the plant?

Andy took out his throw-away cell phone to call Curt. Curt was sitting near the bar. He said he'd call back in three minutes after Andy told him what he needed to know.

It was three minutes and a half.

"She isn't here. Neither is he. Milton is in the coffee shop on Elm, less than a block from here."

"Thanks, Curt. I don't know if I should try to get you out here or whether I should wait. Something's going to break. I feel it.

"Who's running the bar?"

"Ready for this?"

"That tone says it's ... Irene?"

"And Opal.

"This gets weirder and weirder."

Curt would go back to Feld's. Andy went around to the side of the plant to see another grey Honda parked next to the storage shed, out of sight.

Timmins, Walker, Bertstein, Seyers and Price were inside the plant. Fannie was now standing out front. She saw Andy and waved, then put her palms up and shrugged. Manners saw that and opened the car door to look back to where Andy was standing. He got out and they went together by the door to the plant.

"Seyers and Sam went in at eight minutes to six. The others came out at six. They never came back, so I went in. I couldn't find them. They aren't in any of the offices or labs in the front. Bertstein's working in his office. Nobody else in the front part.

"Andy, Millie got a phone call and started running around like a crazy woman. She put Opal in charge – and Opal doesn't know a damned thing about running a bar – and Irene to wait on customers. It's the time some of the people who work here stop for a cool one on their way home.

"What's going on?"

"I wish to hell I knew! Is Timmins in there where you could see her?"

"She's surveilling Bertstein's wife," Manners said. "She called me about twenty minutes ago. They're on their way back from Landsdale."

"Really? I have to talk to you. Her car's right around behind the shed over there." He pointed.

Manners set his jaw. "Now I'm getting really pissed! I have to depend on my partner. I want to know why she's here. I want to know why she's lying to me. It's not the first time!"

"Someone's coming!" Curt hissed. They stepped to the side, behind the large podocarpus. A few seconds later Timmins came to carefully peer around the door toward Manners' car. She stepped back and went inside and to the large window to the side toward where her car was parked. They were able to watch her through the little window by the door. She opened the window and was able to barely squeeze through.

Manners set his jaw again and stepped around the corner to greet her.

She argued a minute, then sighed. "How did you find me?"

"You surely didn't think they would trust you anymore than me?" he replied with a sneer. "I've had it with this bullshit routine! I'm a millimeter from walking out of here! I'm gonna get some answers or all hell is gonna to rain down on this idiotic farce of an assignment!

"Straight! As you know it! Now!"

"Let's go somewhere. I want an answer or two, myself!" she returned. "I want to know if this is as dangerous as it's beginning to look. Nothing is like they said. I want to know what that damned bank has to do with it!"

"Bank?" Manners asked, confused. That was something new to Andy, too.

"I get orders from Gilders, the big shit at the Downleavy Bank and Trust on Oak. Did the agency open a damned *bank* to run an operation? It's insane!"

Somebody is!" Curt said acidly.

A Confused Mess

They sat around in the station with coffee. Fannie gave a report and went to watch the bar for Millie and Sam's return. Curt would go to Feld's. Herndon was off shift and had stayed because there was no one else.

"First off, the whole bit about the agency. What are they pulling here? What's this shit about you spying on me and lying to me?" Manners demanded. "I mean it about no more shit."

"I don't know! I got a coded from HQ that said to meet with Gilders at that little excuse for a bank to receive orders and to not let you know about it."

"You met with Gilders?" Andy asked. "What did he have to say?"

"That there was infiltration on this end. They said Gene didn't know anything about it and wasn't suspected, but that he was being used by a phony setup of some kind. The tip-off was meeting with Feld. You know how suspicious they are of him."

"Feld? I didn't meet with Feld! Andy did!"

"So. Gilders is the phony. He wants to see what's going on. What else did you tell him?" Andy asked.

"Nothing. He said to be very careful around you and Curt. Millie was a special agent investigating Milton, who has some kind of connection with a couple of hoods in Landsdale. There's a really big drug deal here. The bacteria thing is a very small test lab, nothing more."

"Ah!" Manners cried. "The agency didn't even suspect the

bacteria project! I deliberately didn't report on it except to say there might be a side issue involved!"

"And Millie is the head honcho on this end," Andy finished. "There would be no other reason for him to be brought up unless it was an attempt to draw suspicion away from Millie."

"So. You were there. What was Millie up to, with whom?" Manners asked.

"She met Walker. They went to Bertstein's office, then his wife went with them to the back. I couldn't get close enough to hear anything, even if it wasn't insulated. I couldn't see anything.

"Bertstein went back into his personal lab section. The rest were in the packaging section. There's an office back there, I think."

The phone lit up. Andy picked it up, said who he was, then wrote a couple of lines, said to get to the car and have the motor running. He called Curt and said to get to the Walbert plant. Fast!

He ran outside and jumped into the waiting car.

"What the hell, now?" Timmins asked.

"Bertstein's acting a little prematurely. I hope he doesn't lose the really big ones on this!"

They screamed into the plant. The sliding gates were shut, but the man guarding saw them coming and opened them quickly. They ran for the entrance and inside, where Mory was sitting on a marble bench in the reception room. He had an atomizer bottle on his lap.

"I decided to wait until you were here so you can hear and see what was going on. I didn't realize Laine was in charge of anything like this. I swear to you I would have stopped it, even if I had to kill her to do it.

"They had me package the spliced cultures. They are far enough along to ensure the process can continue. They said that the government men would pick up the cultures tonight and the search that is scheduled for tomorrow morning will find nothing more than standard drug resistant isolation chambers we use to produce new drugs.

"Millie sent that Sam person to watch me. She told him to kill me as soon as everything was packaged. She didn't know I was on the other side of the partition.

"I offered him some apple juice while he waited when we were in back. He was in the sterile entrance and I closed it off. He was dead in less than four minutes. It was horrible!

"It is time they come to look for me. I brought the real cultures here. We will have some answers very soon.

"I ask that you don't come closer than ten feet to me at any time. They will be in front of me, you will be behind. I am not sure if this will help or hinder, but swear to you this research will be totally destroyed as soon as it serves its purpose here."

Sue started to say something at the same time Gene did. Andy put up a hand.

"Mory, it will be better to give them something to deliver to whoever comes for it. I figure someone is on the way is why the gate was so easy to open. The old man there was expecting someone and was opening it before we were quite there.

"It will be fast. Can you fix up something?"

"I suppose, but why?"

"So we get them all. Everyone here is taking orders from someone else. Millie is the head of it, but there are others up higher. I want them exposed for what they are."

Mory grinned dryly. "These are false. I would never chance

letting something like this get away. I didn't know if you would try to stop me and was only going to scare you with this. We can let them have this!"

"How do we get them to give it to the delivery?" Sue asked.

A car drove up out front. "That will be the delivery man," Gene said.

A distinguished man came in the door. He stopped short when he saw Sue.

"Welcome to Walbert Research, Mr. Gilders," Sue said, smirking. "I think perhaps Mr. Bertstein has something for you?"

She turned to Mory with wide eyes and a slight pucker of the lips only he could see. He nodded very slightly.

"For me? Whatever...?"

Mory pointed the atomizer nozzle at Gilders. "It's a little genetic insert experiment. I can say with certainty it works to specs. We will now go through the door behind and to the left of me. Do not hesitate or question me. You will die – horribly – to regret it!

"Officers, please stay behind me at all times. I beg in the name of God that you not do anything to make me release what's in this jar." He pointed to the door with the nozzle. Gilders was actually staggering. He was sobbing and trying to speak, but couldn't more than squeak.

"I suppose you saw those things on TV about this kind of thing," Mory continued. "I can assure most definitely, as you will shortly see, that they underplayed the reality."

They went to the hallway behind a desk and in to a door with a small glass panel.

"Do not attempt to open the door. It will not open. Just look through the glass. That was Samuel Price. He got one drop of what's in here on his foot when he dropped a phial.

Gilders looked pleadingly at them. Mory said to look. Now!

Gilder's shakily peered through the glass, then gasped, choked, and vomited.

"That took four minutes. I imagine it seemed like four years to him," Mory continued. "You will now answer any and all questions these officers ask you. You will not falter nor hesitate. You will be absolutely truthful and will conceal not one simple fact.

"I hope you clearly understand?

"I am doing this on my own advice. My wife was used in this scheme. I fully intend to end my agony anyhow. I do not wish to bring anyone, even such as you, into it, but I will not hesitate to do so.

"You will stay in front of me. The officers will stay...!"

The door behind them flew open and Millie and Walker charged in, coming to a sudden halt. Laine came in a few seconds later to see them all staring at Mory and Gilders.

"This is your plague. Mr. Gilders will tell you it works as expected. I won't hesitate to use it on you. You will move to stand with Mr. Gilders," Mory ordered. They hesitated. Millie started to say something. Mory pushed the pressure plunger and pointed the nozzle at them.

They moved to stand with Gilders.

"Mory, Honey, what's going on? Have you gotten some of one of your little personal projects out of hand? We can help you, dear. Put the jar down."

"That's the first time you called me 'Honey' or 'Dear' in three years. It's too late for that now.

"You and I will not leave this room alive if the information these officers seek is not forthcoming and accurate. I do not wish to continue with what you have put on my consciousness, my very soul.

"You sold me to hell. You're going with me. It will be your choice if it is now or after you have had some time to try to atone for your greed.

"Officer Betts, I think you will want to know who is in charge of this travesty and where they can be found? And some proof?" He turned to where Andy could see his face. He winked. "And one other thing. If I am forced to pull this lever, stay as far behind me as possible and get out that door in two seconds or less. To ascertain you are safe, if you are not immediately affected, take two of the yellow capsules in my brown leather case under the bench where I was seated when you entered. Take another two in four hours, even if you are not affected. It is tetracycline and will be effective if taken rapidly enough.

"Laine, Honey and Dear, answer the question. Who? Where?"

She set her jaw and stared at him. He squeezed the lever until a very fine mist barely made contact with her. She screamed and tried to run, but there was a wall behind her.

Mory had two yellow capsules in his hand. He held them out to her. She grabbed at his hand. "Who?" he demanded, closing his hand over the capsules.

"Auermond! Francis Auermond! Paris!" she screeched. He gave her the capsules, which she tossed down quickly.

"I think the tetracycline was in time," Mory said calmly. "Andy? Next question?"

"Contact in Landsdale?"

He pointed the nozzle at Millie.

"Mannie Lewis, me. Lyle Turpin, Laine. We all reported to

Laine first.

"My God! We answered the questions! Get that stuff away from me!"

"Mr. Gilders, who do you report to?" Andy asked.

He sobbed and gasped. Mory pointed the nozzle at him. He squealed and passed out.

"Mory, I think we can expect answers from them now. Please don't take chances with that stuff anymore," Manners said. "They will answer our questions and the answers will prove out or we will simply announce that they answered the ones that do prove out and suggest they answered all of them, then let them go."

"Let them *go*?!" Mory cried.

"What their, er, confederates will do to them would make the stuff in that bottle the easy way out," Sue replied. "Don't take chances with that stuff. Please!"

"I will keep it here until we have them delivered and in a secure cell," Mory replied. "I will then dispose of it and decontaminate any possible area where any of it may survive, if you will be so kind as to delay my encarcelment until such is accomplished?"

"Under the circumstances, I'll agree," Andy answered. "I'll seek a warrant that implies you were acting under extreme duress and were not responsible for the death of Sam Price. After all, he broke the vial and spilled the stuff on himself. You immediately isolated the germ to stop it from contaminating the whole damned town!"

Sue got a cup of cold water from the dispenser to throw in Gilder's face. The whole bunch were herded to the FBI cars and were crowded in when there was a commotion just past the fence. Gilders went down and there was a shot from the area. Curt called that he got the one who shot at them. Andy ran over to find Lyle Turpin laying on the ground next to the podocarpus by the gate. There was a rifle with a silencer on it by his hand.

"I shot as soon as I could. I think he got a shot off," Curt said.

"Gilders. I don't know how bad," Andy replied. "Call Doc for this one and tell him not to go into the plant. Price's body's in there. Don't go anywhere near it. They have those plastic suits to use getting him out and decontaminating the chamber. Mory can direct that."

"Mory? Wasn't he one of them?"

"He was the one who exposed them and got our answers for us. I have to talk with Sue and Gene, then we're done with this end of it, I think. Lewis will probably admit to trafficking to avoid what will happen to him if he blabs a word about this part."

They called Doc and Anne, then headed for the station.

When everyone was booked and in cells, Mory had gone with Curt to help Doc and Anne with Price (they had taken care of Turpin while the booking was going on) Andy took Sue and Gene into his office. They sat around, exhausted, with the horrible coffee in the office urn.

"Okay. Auermond," Andy said.

"I called Richmond," Sue replied. "They'll have Carmody call as soon as he can get in. This is really big. They knew there was such a place and such a group working on this shit, but we found it and will get the credit for the capture.

"They didn't like me demanding Andy and Curt share equal credit. They want it all in the agency."

"We all want things we'll never have," Gene said.

"Carmody's liason with Interpol, Andy. I wonder how they'll manage to make it all FBI and only the last clean-up anyone else."

"They won't," Sue said, smirking. "It involves Israel, officially or not. They'll put it all on Interpol and some hick cops. They'll claim we were called in for the clean-up and not much more. They don't want to let people see where there were some telling tie-ins the conspiracy groups will have a field day with!"

"But Mory's Jewish and he's the one who brought it to a head and exposed what they were doing!"Andy cried. "He's like most Jews! Those extremists are only a very few!"

"They're in charge of a lot of things. All the conspiracy people will see is that the main contact here was a Jewish *banker*! That's what all Jews are about! Money!" Sue said.

Andy couldn't deny that would happen. It's a very sad world we live in.

A Victory Party

"That was some mess!" Art said, shaking his head. "Trying to get them deported? They were American citizens! How the hell do you deport anyone to the country they were never out of?"

"We'll be re-assigned to another case," Gene said. "I think I'll miss this town. It's kind of nice."

"Maybe it'll be tranquil for the next fifty years," Anne said. "I doubt you'll need a head of forensics here. I sure learned a lot more than they teach you in the university! Curt knows more about the field work than any professor I ever had!"

Curt hugged her a bit tighter. They had decided they liked each other.

"I kept thinking it was Millie Seyers all the way. She was one cold customer," Curt replied. "I never did figure exactly where Feld was in it."

"He was a dupe," Andy said. "He was a distraction. Millie admitted he was her idea. She had him investigating her, he would never find anything. Anyone who came here looking into anything would see him as not fitting, so would concentrate on him. I almost did for the first ten minutes.

"It was all about money. If they had what they actually did develop, they could collect billions from several countries. They wouldn't dare to let one have it or it would be used, sooner or later. The Zionist part was just to sell it to them for all the billions, then they could hold it over the heads of everyone else.

"Mory has the whole drug company now. I think he should

get a citizenship medal. He really did think it was to be so we would have a defense if someone else developed it. It didn't occur until lately that there isn't a defense. There wouldn't be time to get a serum or immunity program in effect when the stuff killed in minutes. It would necessarily be an offensive weapon. When he figured that, he did something to put an end to it.

"I loved it when we were here at booking and he dumped his jar down the sink. Laine would have clawed him to death if she could have reached him. It was only water.

"You say Millie was cold? Laine was ten times colder!

"They're the type who define Zionists. The end justifies the means.

"It almost never does."

"And the world rolls along as always," Art added.

"I'll have a tequila and grapefruit on ice," Andy said. "I'm off duty and I deserve a drink."

They all agreed he deserved at least that. They also agreed it was time to change the subject – even if they didn't say it.

C. D. Moulton's works are available on most major outlets as printed or e-books. CD writes the CD Grimes, PI, mysteries, the Det. Lt. Nick Storie mysteries, the Clint Faraday mysteries, the Flight of the Maita science fiction series, books on orchid culture and many others of many types. Mystery, adventure, intrigue, science fiction, humor, fantasy, paranormal, mild erotica, and factual.